I0728753

THE
MOUNTAIN

SAMMY HANMER-WOODS

The Mountain
© Sammy Hanmer-Woods 2025

All rights reserved. No part of this publication may be reproduced, stored in a retrieval system, or transmitted in any form or by any means, electronic, mechanical, photocopying, recording or otherwise, without the prior written permission of the author.

Sammy Hanmer-Woods is recognised as the creator of this content and has asserted the right to be identified as the author of this work.

ISBN: 978-1-923512-95-5 (Paperback)

A catalogue record for this book is available from the National Library of Australia

Cover Design: Sammy Hanmer-Woods and Clark & Mackay
Format and Typeset: Sammy Hanmer-Woods and Clark & Mackay
Published by Sammy Hanmer-Woods and Clark & Mackay

Proudly printed in Australia by Clark & Mackay

Chapter 1

The boy stood at the foot of the mountain.

"Come help me with the chores," his mother called.

Chores were nothing new to him; they began in the village from a very early age. As in most villages, the older you grew, the more tasks you had and the more complex your jobs became. The boy had never known a life without chores.

The boy had lived in the village his whole life and was now situated on the brink of adulthood. Strangers often passed through the village. They sold essential supplies, they sometimes aided in the chores, and they spun yarns. The boy had seldom left the village. He had been to a few neighbouring towns, but they weren't all that different from the village in which he and his family resided. The salesmen and the labourers that came to visit had been most everywhere, it seemed. They told tales of adventure and exhilaration. The boy wanted to feel those things. The men who visited had experienced love. They spoke of passion and powerful emotions. Sometimes, during arguments with his parents or the other village children, the boy caught a glimpse of the emotions that the men described. He felt the heat in their cheeks and the sweat on their necks, as if his own face were burning—as if his own neck were dripping.

He had spoken to one man, many years prior, who told tales about the loss of a dear friend. He had loved this friend very much; they were both painters. The man had journeyed to the town of the boy in an attempt to sell some of their paintings. The boy lived in a modest hut where no art was hung. He had never seen such colours as the ones displayed in the paint. He recognised the blue from the sky and the deep green from the hills, but never had he seen such vibrant reds. He expressed this to the painter, to which the painter replied, "Few people have seen a red this strong. Few people have known these colours."

"Please," said the boy, "I want never to forget this colour red." The man said to him, "You will see much red in your life."

"When?" asked the boy.

A wry smile crept across the man's lips. "I cannot promise you when you will see the red. I almost wish you won't." The painter looked down at the floor as he finished his sentence. He had with him many paintings.

"Why did you bring your art here if you don't want me to see the red?" said the boy. The man repeated his gestures—a cheeky smile followed abruptly by diverted eye contact. He reached towards one of the smallest paintings he had.

"I want you to see the red," he intimated.

That was the first and last time the boy had ever seen the painter. He kept with him the small painted red square that he had been given. It had lived under his bed for many years. In all the time that had passed since the boy's inter-action with the painter, he still had never wit-nessed such a vibrant red as the one in the paint. He wished to.

"What's on the other side of the mountain?" the boy inquired of his mother one afternoon. "How should I know?" she replied.

"Aren't you curious?"

"That mountain is too steep to climb."

The boy looked up at the mountain. It *was* steep. "Has anyone ever climbed it?" he said.

"I don't know," his mother replied. She could not have been more unhelpful.

Chapter 11

The boy's curiosity would not go away. That night, he asked his father if anyone had ever climbed the mountain. His father had many friends. They often laughed together at a volume that the boy himself had never laughed. The boy had a few friends of his own, but they never laughed in the way that the men laughed. The boy had made the mistake of asking his father a serious question while his father was surrounded by men who wanted to be anything but serious. The father's friends leapt to life at such a question. "Oh, I know a man who's climbed a mountain!" cried one of them.

"I know a man who's climbed *ten* mountains!" exclaimed another.

"But has anyone climbed *this* mountain?" asked the boy.

The men fell silent. They looked around at each other. Finally, his father said, "I've never known a man to climb that mountain."

Weeks passed, and the boy could not get the mountain off his mind. Was there a point to climbing it? His desire began to consume him.

When the boy was very young, he was a happy child. He loved learning from the people who passed through the village, but never was he envious of them. Never did he begrudge them the fact that their eyes had seen what his had not. But increasingly, he was growing angry with his own eyes. He wished they could see more than what was directly in front of them.

The weeks turned into months, and the boy's eyes saw not nearly as many new things as he yearned for. He was getting to the age where he *knew* of all the chores. He knew all the options that awaited him in the village. The available jobs were not boring in themselves, but they were boring compared to the mountain. Still, he worked hard. He did his best at the tasks presented to him, and he completed every job that came his way. His desire to ascend the peak grew so great that it served as his daily motivation. All through his work, he fantasised about the view from the top. He wondered if the painter from all those years ago had ever climbed a mountain. Were there really men who had climbed *ten* mountains?

Surely that wasn't true.

One night, the boy was sitting on his bed after an arduous day of work. He reached for the painting that had inhabited the floor beneath him for so long. The redness was taunting him.

No man from my village has ever seen this colour red, he thought to himself. *I bet my father has never seen this red.* The boy loved his father. He was a good man. He had a laugh that was unrivalled and a loyal pack of hyenas who were always quick to share in his levity. *But my father has never seen this red,* thought the boy.

Chapter III

The boy's craving for the mountain grew stronger and stronger to the point where it scared him. *Why is this mountain so important to me?* he wondered. *Why can't I be happy with my role here in the village like everyone else?* His desire worried him so much that he was too afraid to speak of it. His friends and acquaintances didn't seem to care about what might await them above. All they ever spoke about were chores. There were some nice girls in the village, but they seemed to care about the mountain even less than his friends. The girls talked to each other with a level of sincerity that the boy had never before witnessed. They talked effusively about how they viewed one another—that was more than the boy could say for his friends. The girls saw only what was in front of them, but they understood it in a way that the boy's friends did not. *I would never distract the girls with the idea of the mountain,* he thought to himself. *They are happy as they are; they want for nothing more than what they have.* His peers' lack of interest in the mountain angered him. He wished that they shared his passion. He wished he could be as satisfied as they were.

The boy's longing for the summit that had so cruelly eluded him reached its one-year birthday. So many thoughts had raced through the boy's mind during the past annum. More often than not, he reprimanded himself for his obstinate desire. He wished he could be present and enjoy his chores for what they were instead of letting his mind wander to something that he might never attain. *How does one even go about climbing a mountain?* he had asked himself. It's not something that he truly wished to do alone, but from the few people he had spoken to, no-one seemed to crave it as desperately as he did. His mother couldn't care less about the potential of the zenith. She was okay with what she didn't know, residing in the fact that the apex was beyond her comprehension. His father was fulfilled by his friends, something for which the boy admired him. Other boys his age were consumed by their jobs, eager to be the quickest and the strongest at completing their tasks. And the girls he knew valued each other too much to risk losing what they had for the possibilities of the mountain. The boy began to despise himself, not just for what he couldn't see, but for the fact that he may never see it.

All the neighbouring villages knew of each other. The boy had made past voyages with his father to purchase supplies for their village. His father was an adroit builder and often constructed things with his friends. One day, the men were short on materials. "Don't worry," said one of his father's friends. "I know a man a few towns away who can provide us with what we need—he can even help us build the next set of homes." The men and the boy waited patiently for the friend to make contact with the man that he knew. It took weeks for the man's friend to eventually reach the boy's settlement. The man brought with him the necessary provisions. He also brought his daughter.

Chapter IV

The boy bided time with his father on the day that the man and his daughter were set to arrive, ready to help with the imminent construction. His father, being the gracious and gregarious man that he was, invited the newcomers in for dinner upon their advent. The boy's father was a diligent man, even if not desirous. The boy had once inquired about his father's work ethic.

"What drives you to work so well?" the boy had asked.

"I work to provide for you and your mother," his father matter-of-factly replied.

"Did you work hard before you knew us?" the boy questioned.

"My work is easy because I laugh," said his father.

"What about when you are not laughing?" questioned the boy.

"That is when the hard work begins."

***

The boy's mother and father had hosted many a dinner party. His mother had friends too. They also laughed, but their jokes weren't as funny to the boy. And they weren't as grounded with their laughter. The laughter of his father's friends seemed to bring them closer to the earth. But the laughter of his mother's friends took them somewhere else entirely. Perhaps, closer to the mountain of their choosing.

The dinner that his parents hosted for the father and daughter was nothing that the boy hadn't witnessed before. He often grew quiet at these dinners. He observed and rarely contributed. That night was no different. The girl didn't seem so dissimilar to the other girls that he knew. He supposed the only visible difference between her and the girls he had previously perceived was that this particular girl was alone. He rarely saw girls alone. They were always so intertwined with one another. Not necessarily in a physical sense—their connection to one another was discernible even when they were not touching. The boy knew not one single girl who would leave the friends of her village to travel with her father. The boy wondered what had possessed this girl to leave such a presumably close circle.

As the night went on, the boy made a desultory attempt to speak with the girl. His mother and father were sitting with the man at the other end of the table, and the boy had grown restless watching a play in which he held no part. He turned to the girl. "What brings you here?" he asked.

"Curiosity," she replied.

The hair on the back of the boy's neck instantly stood up. "Don't you have friends at home?" he asked.

"I have friends everywhere," she replied with a smile.

What an odd thing to say, he thought to himself. *No-one has friends everywhere.*

The adults continued talking, and the young pair stepped outside. The boy felt an almost unsettling sense of normalcy with her. It was a bizarre thing to feel when in the presence of a stranger.

"Have you ever climbed a mountain?" he asked.

"No," she replied.

"Why not?"

"Why would I climb a mountain?"

"I've always wanted to."

"Then you should."

The pair had been strolling, and he stopped to look at her. "You don't think it's strange to climb a mountain?" he asked.

"What's strange about that?"

"I've never known anyone who wants to climb a mountain," the boy stated.

"I've never known anyone with a reason to," she replied curtly.

The boy didn't know what to make of her.

"Have you ever met anyone else who's wanted to climb a mountain?" he probed.

"No, I have not," she said. "But I have never met a lot of people. You think you are the only one out there who wants to climb a mountain?"

The boy did think that.

"I've never known anyone who wants to climb a mountain," he repeated. "How long are you staying here?" he asked her.

"As long as it takes for the buildings to be constructed. I won't help the men build, but I will help the other women with their chores."

"Do you really have friends everywhere?" he asked.

"Everywhere I have been," she responded.

"Where have you been?"

"Everywhere," the girl said with a grin. "You ask too many questions," she stated. "I'm going back to the house."

Chapter V

The girl and her father moved in with the friend who had invited them. Weeks passed, and the forming of the new houses was well underway. The boy helped his father build, and the girl began to aid the other women with their jobs.

"I must ask you again why you came here," inquired the boy.

"To learn," replied the girl.

"Do you feel you are learning?"

"Every day. The work here is not so different from the work where I am from, but the people are different."

"How are they different?"

"They've seen different things. The soil is richer here; the plants grow stronger and brighter. It's too early to tell whether the women are stronger and brighter too. I think they seem brighter because I have gazed for too long at the lights back home. You grow tired of the same lights after basking in their glow for too long."

The boy understood what she meant. "I want to climb the mountain," he said.

"Why?" she probed.

"I have gazed at the plants here for too long. My eyes yearn for what they have not seen, and my heart yearns for what it has not felt."

"What do you think you will find at the top of this mountain?" she said.

"I don't know. And that is why I must climb it."

There was a pause.

"Will you climb the mountain with me?" he asked.

"Before I met you, I had never known any-one who wished to climb a mountain. I myself have never wished for that…."

"Will you climb the mountain with me?" he repeated.

"I will."

Chapter VI

The mountain was not particularly jagged and did not present any immediate threat of injury. It was, however, very vast, high, and steep.

"How does one go about climbing a mountain?" the girl said.

This was a question that the boy had asked himself countless times.

"I think we need a blessing," the boy responded. "There is no way for us to carry all the food, water, and shelter that we would require. The priestess can bless us."

"Why have you never attempted to climb the mountain until now?" the girl asked.

"I have never had anyone to climb it with."

***

The priestess's hut was far more ornately decorated than its neighbouring homes. There had once been a collection of religious figures who provided the villagers with their blessings.

The group had consisted of two other women and a man, but the other two women and the man had since passed, leaving the sole remaining priestess. The boy seldom entered any religious building. It was rare that he required a blessing. Most everything that he needed already abounded, and everything that he desired first required his own permission before he could seek anyone else's. That day, he decided to grant himself the freedom to, at the very least, attempt to quash his persistent and painful ardency.

"We require a blessing," he pronounced to the priestess. The boy, his father, the girl, and her father now stood in the sacred dwelling. The boy's father did not truly understand his son's desire to ascend the precipitous peak, but he was an indulgently civil man. The girl's father had entered the village merely to build. He knew well of his daughter's curiosity and knew better than to discourage it.

"I bless you with the grace you require to ascend the mountaintop. May your care and fondness for one another carry you to the limits of the precipice. I know not what you will see."

The uncertainty in the room was palpable. The words "care and fondness" struck the boy. He had known the girl only a number of weeks. He was fond of the poise with which she handled her uncertainty. Her curiosity seemed not a burden to her. It was strange to him that even the priestess knew not what was at the top of the mountain. He presumed the priestess's wisdom to be far greater than his, but perhaps her wisdom lay in the earnestness of her humble confession.

The boy and the girl looked at each other and then at their parents. The apogee awaited.

Chapter VII

The first few days of the trek went by quickly.

"I want to know more about what brought you to the village," said the boy. "I want to know more of the lands you have seen."

"I have not seen many lands," said the girl. "I have not truly been everywhere, but I have made friends everywhere I have been. I may not have truly seen everything, but everything I have seen has truly seen me. There are pieces of me left in every place I have travelled to. The funny thing about leaving pieces of yourself behind is that the pieces always grow back. I show as many sides of myself as I can to the lands I see, and I leave behind the parts of me they will appreciate."

"Were you unhappy in your home village?" asked the boy.

"Not initially. My father enjoys having me as a travel companion, and I became enamoured with the lands I saw while I was away from home. You cannot unsee what you have seen, but what you have seen can help you perceive what you are yet to witness."

They walked in silence for seconds that seemed like minutes. "Were you unhappy in your village?" asked the girl.

"I was unhappy with the lack of curiosity I felt from those around me, which led me to admonish the curiosity I felt within myself. When you are the only person asking questions, you begin to wonder if the answers are worth pursuing."

"The answers are worth pursuing," she responded.

Chapter VIII

"Tell me your fears," said the boy.

"I fear that what I have seen in the past will prevent me from enjoying what is yet to be seen in my future."

The boy could not understand this. He feared the opposite. He feared that what he was yet to see was preventing him from appreciating his past.

"How does this affect how you feel in the present?" he said.

"I live solely for the present. I know not how to understand my past, and the future holds even less clarity."

The boy admired the girl. He admired how she spoke with noticeable honesty. He admired how quick she was to acknowledge her faults. But what he could not admire was the fact that she held no desire to explain her faults. She held no detectable desire to understand her past, and the boy knew that the key to enjoying the future lay in understanding one's past.

Chapter IX

The landscape that the boy viewed whilst climbing the mountain was not yet so different to the landscape seen in the village. The vegetation was sparser, though, and the viridescence more dull.

"What is your favourite plant?" asked the boy.

"There are beautiful flowers in the village I am from that bloom miniature red buds."

"You have seen the red?!" exclaimed the boy.

"Of course I have seen the red," responded the girl. "The red flowers grow close to the pink ones. I suppose the red is not my favourite; they are both my favourite, because they grow together. There are some plants in nature that help each other grow. I could never admire the red if the pink was not also there."

The boy was becoming progressively aware that the girl had seen much more than he had seen. He resolved not to judge her for her past. He could never understand the things about her that she was yet to understand of herself.

"Who is your favourite painter?" he asked.

"I don't know any painters," she said. "Do you?"

The boy told her about the painter he had met all those years ago. He told her of his coveted red square and his infinite desire to see such vibrancy replicated in real life. He told her that his eyes yearned for that which his heart had already glimpsed.

"How can your heart catch a glimpse of something that your eyes have never seen?" she asked.

"Many men have passed through my village. They have told me tales of passion. Stories of agony and euphoria, fear and depression. I have borne witness to nary a circumstance that elicits the intensity of which these men speak. It is a curse to feel as others feel. I may not have seen what those men have seen, but my heart beats as if it were in the chest of a man whose eyes I do not share."

Chapter X

The plants on the mountain had begun to contrast with the plants in the village. The village provided a perpetual smorgasbord of lush greens, whereas the verdancy of the mountain was much more scattered, much more inconsistent. There were fewer flowers on the mountain, but the flowers that did abound were much more lurid than the petals to which the boy was accustomed.

"Have you ever been drunk?" asked the girl.

"I'm sorry?" said the boy.

"Many villages I have been to have taverns. They are lively and brimming with the passion you speak of."

"Intoxication is not passion," replied the boy.

"I would love to drink at one of those taverns. I looked through the windows one time and I saw a woman dancing on one of the tables. As she twirled, her hair engulfed her body. Her smile was the widest one I have ever discerned."

"My father drinks sometimes. He does not, however, drink as much as his friends. My father can make people laugh even when he is not drinking, but his friends often have to be drunk to make him laugh. One of my father's friends got so drunk once that he threw up in our garden. Up until then, the friend had been laughing raucously. After the alcohol left his body, he scarcely made an utterance. Perhaps I would be funnier if I drank, or perhaps my body would regorge itself of laughter entirely."

The pair continued on their upward traipse. The boy was noticing more and more the disparity between the colours of the plants on the mountain and the colours of the plants in the village. The flowers on the mountain held the richest hues he had ever seen. Luminous yellows and brilliant purples. He wasn't sure how many of these plants were edible. He assumed that, because the priestess had blessed them with all they needed to survive, no ingestible plants bothered to present themselves. Even though he never ate any of the flowers that he saw, he was conscious of how much they satiated him. Just gazing at their brightness left him feeling fuller than most meals he had ever consumed. The girl wandered towards a nearby shrub. Its leaves were a deep green and they housed tiny white florets.

From the leaves hung an assortment of violet-tinted fruits. The girl picked one and drew it to her lips.

"Don't do that!" cried the boy.

"We have been blessed; no harm can come to us."

The boy paused for a moment. He wasn't sure if that was true. The priestess's words echoed through his mind—*May your care and fondness for one other carry you to the limits of the precipice.*

"We must care for one another," he said.

"I came on this journey to learn," she asserted. "Who are you to stop me from learning?"

"Please," the boy urged, "pick the fruit but eat it later. We are too early into our journey to have any harm befall us." He wasn't sure if that was true either. Verily, he wasn't sure how far into their journey they were at all. But he knew it was too early to lose her. The girl heeded his plea and placed the fruit into her shirt pocket. They ventured onwards.

Chapter XI

———

"What is the most dangerous fruit you have ever consumed?" the boy inquired.

"When I was a child, I was on an exploit with my father. It is probably the most daring escapade I have ever undertaken. We voyaged so far south that we reached the sea."

The boy had never been to the sea.

"I had never seen the sea before, and I haven't seen it since. My father never took me back after what happened. I ingested a sea-fruit so deadly that it rendered me speechless. My father beseeched me to speak, but I could not. He always says that the waves stole my words. I got them back eventually, but never again in my life have I been silenced in the way that the sea silenced me. Never before had I marvelled at the magnitude and ferocity of such a force. Never again has nature bequeathed upon me something so breathtaking that my words become superfluous."

And just like that, the girl became the ocean to the boy. He knew not what to say to her. He had never even left the province, let alone felt his eyes gape at the soporific savagery of the sea. He had never eaten a dangerous fruit; he had never met a woman who had. He wished in that moment to consume the entire bush-full of indigo-painted fruits that they had previously seen in the hope of understanding the girl on a more visceral level.

"I would return to the sea if I could," said the girl. "I have often daydreamed about being dumbfounded again in the way that I once was. Being rendered speechless by a force that allures you rather than repels you is one of the most enlivening things that a soul can experience."

Chapter XII

The girl began to feel about the boy in opposition to how she had once felt about the ocean. When she was with him, she spoke at a frequency that alarmed her. She had met many men and many boys who had informed her of the beauty she possessed. *How can they think I am beautiful?* she would ask herself. *They don't even know me.*

The girl began to become enamoured with the boy's curiosity. His roving mind and spirit had enraptured her. The girl's father was also a streeler; he went from place to place accumulating memories like a museum collecting art. She knew her father well enough to have roamed through the art-filled corridors of his mind. Despite the apparent inquisitive nature of the boy's pneuma, she observed that the motive of his curiosity was different to that of her father's. The boy voyaged to appreciate all he had left behind. He disdained his own eyes more than he derided what they had seen. The girl's father, although having a comprehensive understanding of the places from which he digressed, never looked back. He felt he had unassailable reasoning for leaving behind each place he had once enjoyed, and thus never desired to return. The girl knew the boy would one day return to his village with a new-found cognisance, but her father would never return to the towns he had once deserted—the same way her father would never take her back to the ocean.

The girl's father knew her better than anyone else in the world. When he called her beautiful, she knew that his eyes saw deeper than her skin and perceived the truth of her soul.

Sometimes, the girl grew tired of her father's questions. Although his curiosity was genuine, he often didn't employ the answers he obtained. The girl had witnessed her father make the same mistakes many a time. The two of them travelled from town to town on a horse and carriage. The girl knew how to keep the horses happy. She knew which foods they preferred and where they liked to be petted. The girl's father also knew the horses well, but oftentimes he would pat them in spots that he knew they didn't like. He liked to get a rise out of them.

The horses struggled with uneven terrain. Still, the girl's father sometimes chose to travel routes with large stones. When the horses began to struggle, the girl's father was quick to frustration each time. *He knows they don't like this; why does their discomfort continue to surprise him?* There were other, less rocky paths her father could choose, but her father would not change the roads he wished to take.

Chapter XIII

———

"I want to eat the fruit," said the boy.

The girl also wanted to eat the fruit. She removed it from her pocket and broke it into two pieces. It had not lost any of its vibrancy. In fact, its colours were richer than ever.

"Why now do you want to eat it?" she probed.

"I wish to be rendered speechless by a force that allures me, and you could never repel me."

The pair drew the fruit to their lips and ingested with passionate patience. This was not the first unknown fruit that the girl had risked herself for. This was the first riskful food that the boy had ever consumed.

The pair lay against the surface of the mountain and gazed at the clouds. Neither of them had ever been that close to the clouds before.

"You inspire me," said the girl. "I have ogled the ocean, and I have spent my life in search of things that confound me in the way that the waves once did. I too have desired that rendering into silent submission. I admire your curiosity. I admire your place in your village. I admire the certainty that you hold towards your fate at the summit. I have been rendered speechless by men before, but never have I met somebody who makes me feel I have so much to say. Before I met you, I feared I was relegated to a life of soundless staring. I feared it was my fate to observe and perhaps never to contribute. I have met many passionate souls, but it is a rarity to meet somebody who listens as passionately as they speak, who creates as passionately as they consume. There are too many who prize the intonations of their own questions far more than they cherish the sound of the answers given. Or worse still, they never ask questions to begin with because they hold an unmitigated level of arrogance towards the answers they believe they already possess.

Never have I met a man who is as curious as he is patient, and that is a combination of qualities for which I so deeply revere you."

It was in that moment that the boy realised this woman was perhaps the most beautiful creature he had ever seen. He was, however, intoxicated by the fruit, and knew not how seriously his observations were to be taken. *Intoxication is not passion*, he repeated to himself. Still, he could not remove his eyes from her. Surely a woman that beautiful had known many men and many boys. He was too afraid to dwell on such a thought. He wanted to tell her how much he valued her. He wanted to tell her just how mutual the admiration was, but this was his first time under the influence of an intoxicating fruit, so he knew not what to say.

Chapter XIV

The effects of the fruit eventually wore off, but the boy's feelings for the girl did not change. The boy recalled a story that one of his father's friends had once apprised. The friend had been out drinking one evening in a tavern, a tavern similar to that which the girl had fantasised about. He had met a woman for whom he felt similarly to the way in which the boy felt about the girl. "She was the most gorgeous, intoxicating woman I had ever seen!" the friend exclaimed.

"Or it was just the most gorgeous, intoxicating libation you had ever encountered!" ribbed the boy's father.

"No, no, no—she was captivating," the friend continued. He described the way the woman had danced that evening. He described her the way the girl had described the idol-like figure she saw through the tavern window. "I was beguiled by her movements," said the friend. "I had never seen a woman move so freely. I took her home and my feelings became only affirmed. I married her. She never stopped moving freely.

"Eventually, her desire for liberty took her away from me. You see, I wanted only to be free with this woman, but she needed to be free *from* me. The strongest thing I loved about her became the very reason I lost her. Not once did I expect her to change, but how great a tragedy it is for one's most favourable quality to become their most repellent."

Intoxication is not love, the boy thought to himself. But there he stood. There he walked with the girl, completely sober. He felt his feelings as the truest, purest version of himself. And in his lucid mind, he knew he loved her.

Chapter XV

———

"The clouds are so strange," the boy wondered aloud.

"Indeed, they are," responded the girl.

"I have never been this close to the clouds." The boy professed such a factual statement with a level of emotion that extended beyond the literal meaning of its words. He posed it almost as a question. He wanted the girl to tell him that, yes, now as she walked with him, she felt closer to the *clouds* than ever.

"Me neither," she replied.

Joy! thought the boy. *I am as nuanced to her as she is to me.* He immediately admonished himself for such a thought. Perhaps she truly just meant that she had never seen the clouds from this height.

"The clouds look different from this angle," he persisted.

"Well of course they do," she said.

Goddammit, he thought.

"I have gazed at so many clouds in my life, from a multitude of angles. Each set of clouds helps me to understand the next. You cannot unsee what you have seen, but what you have seen can help you perceive what you are yet to witness," the girl repeated.

The boy wished to know everything about the girl. He wished to see all that her eyes had ever seen, feel everything her heart had ever felt, and divine every piece of wisdom her mind had ever come to know. More than that, he wished to exclusively view each assemblage of clouds he was set to ever witness with her by his side. He felt the best way to ensure they remained observation-partners was to look at the clouds the way she looked at the clouds. When you truly love someone, you begin to see the world through their eyes.

He knew not how to be close to her. He knew not how to compliment her in a way that demonstrated the depth of his love. It was too shallow a statement to verbalise her beauty. He wished never to burden her with his desire.

Chapter XVI

"I love leaves," said the girl. "They flourish, they fall, and they return. As a child, I used to sit at the base of trees and observe the leaves on their descent. I was so invested in which leaves would grace the ground first. It was strange, now that I reflect on it, to have watched their downfall as if it were a race. I have always envied evergreen trees. They feel no need to change seasonally. Their leaves drop with insouciance and new ones smoothly grow. There is no recurring compulsion, no predictable variance—they simply change when they are ready."

The boy knew that he would love the girl through every season of her life.

"It is only recently that I have felt a compulsion to change," he responded. "I suppose, like you, I have longed for adventure. But my parents do not travel—they are content in the village. A specific flock of birds migrate to and from our village each year. As a child, I grew very fond of them. Their feathers housed an affluence of colours, and the vibrancy of their beings was reflected in the songs they sang. I would play with them in the trees and run with them as they flew down to the stream. My mother and I made a habit of spending our days engaging with them. One day, we traipsed down to the familiar verdant patch and I saw not the birds.

"'Where are they?' I asked my mother. 'They have migrated,' she replied. 'The food here will not sustain them over the winter, so they must go in search of new sustenance. Don't worry, they will be back.'

"I suppose, as you have envied the leaves, I have envied the birds. They draw from the village all that they can and then, when they have reached their derivational limits, they leave. They know when to vacate and, equally, they know when to return. I feel that each year, when the birds return, the colouring of their feathers is a little brighter and they sing their songs with new-found levels of confidence. The birds would not appreciate the village if they had never left it, and they would not appreciate the next stage of their voyage if they had not felt the nourishment of their home."

"I seldom return to the places to which I have voyaged," said the girl.

"How can you truly appreciate them if you never return?" inquired the boy.

"I appreciate what I have seen, but I have no desire to see things twice."

"You are missing out," said the boy. "You can stare at the same view for years. The view won't necessarily change—that is out of your control. The true tragedy is never having your eyes change. If you stare at one view for too long, you will grow too accustomed to what you are seeing. One of life's greatest pleasures is returning to an unchanged view with freshly cultivated eyes."

Chapter XVII

The boy and the girl argued sometimes. They were quick to question each other, but never was a question asked with malice. They challenged each other only to enhance themselves, never to diminish, ensnare, or belittle one another. Questioning marred with disparaging intent is the bastardisation of curiosity. Knowledge is always the goal, and knowledge pursued with contempt and hostility is an insult to the attainment of wisdom.

They had both grown to value each other's opinion as much as they valued their own. Their opinions often differed, but they were dichotomous equals. *I would happily be challenged by her for the rest of my life*, thought the boy. *I would, with dignity, be held accountable in her court of law. Let her judgement broaden the scope of my virtue, her inquiries expand the depth of my mind, and her deferential desires enrich the capacity of my heart. And to her I shall extend the same courtesy.*

He thought a lot about passion. He had desired to climb the mountain to perceive with his eyes that which his heart had already glimpsed. He had heard men speak of the passion they felt for women—he was certainly passionate about the girl. He felt he was closer to the red than ever.

The girl also felt passion. She felt herself growing closer and closer to the boy, but she grew no closer to understanding herself.

The boy's passion became too much for him to bear. "May I kiss you?" he asked the girl.

The girl had so many unanswered questions. Her mind desperately raced towards a suggestion of what had brought her to this point. She found no clarity in her existing memories, so she resolved to forge a new one.

"Of course," she replied. The girl felt the boy's hands enclasp the sides of her face as she clutched at his back. She was more confused than ever.

The boy felt a wave of calmness he had never felt before. His body buzzed red, but it was not the red he had envisioned. He had imagined red to be an all-consuming, aching sensation, but that was not how it felt at all. He felt an unprecedented level of tranquillity. "When I kiss you," said the boy, "I understand how it feels for the leaves to fall so softly from the trees, because I fall into your arms with that same gentle ease. Never before have I had such acuity into the migration of the birds or the flowing of a stream. I feel I understand the ocean. I am both the waves and the onlooker. *This* is the kind of feeling that can render a man speechless. I have heard men speak of passion before, but never have I heard such placation described. When I kiss you, I feel I am at one with nature and at peace with the world."

Chapter XVIII

____

The pair voyaged towards the summit, hand in hand. They were so close. *Ambition is a funny thing,* thought the boy. *And how hard it is to discern true desire from foisted expectations.*

As they ascended the peak, the horizon became visible. The terrain was growing increasingly vertiginous the further they clambered, the atmosphere a glowing ruby. The air engulfed them in a wine-coloured hue, and they inhaled the crimson oxygen like it were the intoxicant it so fervently resembled. The boy could taste its sweetness. He breathed it in deeply, letting its scarlet sedation assuage all the anguish he had ever endured.

The pair stood at the crest. The boy gazed with wonder in his eyes at the carmine clouds and the vital vermillion that fell before them. Never in his life at the foot of the mountain could he have imagined such devastating brilliance. The sky blazed above them and beamed onto the geography below. As they marvelled on the zenith, their eyes fell to what lay beneath their beings. It was a village. At a glance, it was strikingly similar to the one in which they had begun their journey, but the boy knew it was different to any place he had ever been.

He grabbed the girl's hand and began his descent to the other side. "Where are you going?" she asked.

"We are going to the other side!"

"I'm not," she said.

The boy paused. "Why not?"

"I said I'd climb this mountain with you; I never said I'd cross to the other side."

"But don't you want to see the glory that lies ahead?!"

"Climbing the mountain was never my dream."

The boy knew not what to say. "I could never have climbed this mountain without you," he whispered. "You have shown me all I have ever wanted to see."

"I have other mountains to climb," said the girl.

"I will climb them with you!" exclaimed the boy.

The girl gave him the most sorrowful look he had ever witnessed on a person's face. Her eyebrows furrowed as she let out an earnest susurration—"I must climb my mountains alone."

The boy could not understand. He stood at the pinnacle of his passion and let his eyes widen at the summit of his desires.

"It was never your dream to cross to the other side of the mountain," said the girl. "It was merely your dream to climb it, to marvel at its cap, to understand its potential. You wanted your eyes to see that which your heart had already glimpsed. Have you achieved your dream?"

"My eyes have seen all that my heart has ever desired, and my heart has never been fuller.

I want to revel in the actualisation of my desires. I want to bask in the lambent, florid glow of passion realised."

"I must climb my mountains alone," the girl repeated.

They stared at each other, gazing at all they were set to forgo. The boy looked at her and saw her in her entirety. When he was with her, he was the most present he had ever been. He thought back to all those times he had spent daydreaming about the mountain while doing his chores. He thought of all the games he had played as a child, chasing the birds and running with the stream. *I know I love her*, he thought, *because when I am with her, I want for nothing.*

He wanted to tell her of his love, but he knew better than to change the mind of a person who was certain of their desires.

"May I kiss you goodbye?" she asked.

"No," he responded softly. He had once kissed her with so much hope in his heart. He could never bring himself to kiss her now that the hope was gone.

She looked at him gently and turned to leave. The boy watched her descend the auspicious landscape until he could discern her shape no longer. He turned back to the view from the ridge and let tears fill his eyes, realising he would have to retrace the mountain they had once climbed together without the very reason he had climbed it. His tears clouded his vision until he could hardly see. When he wiped the tears from his eyes, his view was still blurred. He looked down at what was very nearly the mirror image of his village. He saw rolling hills, similar to the ones in which he worked. Rows of homes, alike to the ones he, his family, and close friends all inhabited. He even discerned a steeple similar to that of the priestess's hut. But he had never seen a village like this. He had never admired scenery under such vibrant luminescence. The boy wept as the sky illuminated a future in which he would never exist.

He felt a hand on his shoulder and spun around to the face of the painter. "You have seen the red," the painter said with a grin.

"Now I understand why you didn't want me to see it," responded the boy.

"Do you regret climbing the mountain?" the painter asked.

The boy thought about this deeply. "If I had never climbed the mountain, I would have spent the rest of my life wondering what awaited me at the top. Now I have seen the red. Now I know my heart was not crazy for craving something my eyes had never witnessed."

The painter gave a thin but sincere smile.

The boy continued, "I feel as though my heart could never have imagined the full potential of the mountain. The girl made me feel things even my own heart could not conjure, and that is why I love her. She expanded my mind and connected my eyes to my soul in a way that I never knew possible. Who will challenge me now? Who will expand my mind? Who will guide my heart to destinations it cannot travel to alone?"

"Did you ever mistreat the girl?" inquired the painter.

"Never!" cried the boy. "I wished only to make her as happy as she made me."

"Then love yourself in the knowledge that you have loved her well. The girl has her own mountains to climb, and she must climb them in solitude for reasons unbeknownst to you and even to herself. You left your village with a good understanding of all you were leaving behind. Perhaps you did not truly appreciate what you were deserting, but you understood why you had to voyage beyond what your eyes had grown too accustomed to perceiving. Not everyone knows why they leave what they leave behind. Not everyone understands where they came from, why they left, or even where they are going. The key to enjoying one's future is understanding one's past."

The boy knew these words well and his tears shed once more. "I don't think I will ever love another as I have loved her."

"If you truly cannot see past her, then learn to see the world through the lens of your love. Let the colour she has shown you paint your world forever. Extend the love you have for her to all those around you. Let it continue to soothe you in a way that you have never before been soothed. True love is a pacifier. It mollifies the deepest desires of your heart by teaching your eyes that all they wish to perceive is perceptible. You can never unlearn the love this woman has shown you. To have loved once is all a man needs."

The boy's tears continued to fall. He knew the painter was right. To have loved once is all a man needs.

www.ingramcontent.com/pod-product-compliance
Lightning Source LLC
Chambersburg PA
CBHW030026200726
48283CB00012B/1339